BUBBLE, THE FISH

NAVY-LOU, THE BIRD IN BLUE

HARVEY, THE MONKEY

PAT, THE CAT

MIA, THE MOUSE

RICK, THE CHICK

ROCKY, THE ROOSTER

HELEN, THE HEN

PIGGY, THE PIG

PEPE, THE PENGUIN

CHUCK, THE DUCK

ROGER, THE BADGER

TED, THE TOAD

OTTO, THE OCTOPUS

FOSSIL IS A CROCODILE WHO LOVES TO GO TO THE BEACH WITH HIS FRIENDS. FROM PEPE THE PENGUIN TO RYAN THE LION TO MOOMOO THE COW, FOSSIL'S FRIENDS JUMP INTO THE WATER AND ENCOURAGE FOSSIL TO JOIN THEM.

CAN YOU FIND, NAME, AND COUNT ALL OF HIS FRIENDS AS THEY PLAY IN THE WATER?

AND WHERE ARE THE THREE SMALL RINGS, THE TWO RACQUETS WITH A BALL, THE FISHING NET, AND THE TWO SHELLS THAT ARE HIDDEN IN THE DRAWINGS?

DON'T FORGET CHEWING GUM, THE SPARROW, ABOARD A TINY BOAT!

Published by
Princeton Architectural Press
A McEvoy Group company
202 Warren Street
Hudson, New York 12534

Visit our website at www.papress.com

First published in France under the title
Nageur comme Fossile
© 2017, hélium / Actes Sud, Paris, France

English edition
© 2019 Princeton Architectural Press

All rights reserved
Printed and bound in China
22 21 20 19 4 3 2 1 First edition

ISBN 978-1-61689-801-4

Princeton Architectural Press is a leading publisher in architecture, design, photography, landscape, and visual culture. We create fine books and stationery of unsurpassed quality and production values. With more than one thousand titles published, we find design everywhere and in the most unlikely places.

No part of this book may be used or reproduced in any manner without written permission from the publisher, except in the context of reviews.

Every reasonable attempt has been made to identify owners of copyright. Errors or omissions will be corrected in subsequent editions.

This book was illustrated using colored pencils and pen.

Editor: Nina Pick
Typesetting: Paula Baver

Special thanks to: Janet Behning, Abby Bussel, Benjamin English, Jan Cigliano Hartman, Susan Hershberg, Kristen Hewitt, Lia Hunt, Valerie Kamen, Jennifer Lippert, Sara McKay, Parker Menzimer, Eliana Miller, Nina Pick, Wes Seeley, Rob Shaeffer, Sara Stemen, Marisa Tesoro, Paul Wagner, and Joseph Weston of Princeton Architectural Press
—Kevin C. Lippert, publisher

Library of Congress Cataloging-in-Publication Data available upon request.

THE QUIET CROCODILE

GOES TO THE BEACH

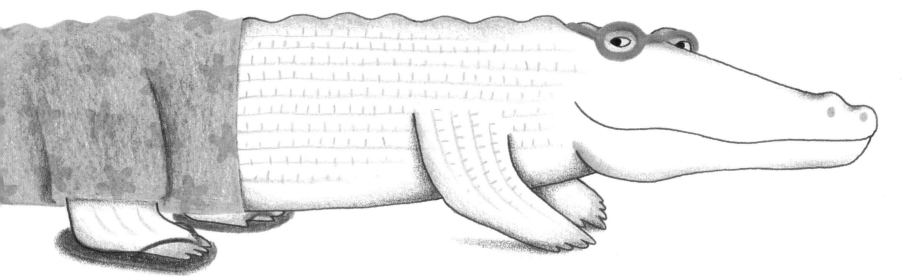

NATACHA ANDRIAMIRADO / DELPHINE RENON

PRINCETON ARCHITECTURAL PRESS · NEW YORK

FOSSIL THE QUIET CROCODILE
LOVES THE BEACH.

HE'S ALWAYS THE FIRST TO ARRIVE
(WELL, ALMOST).

THERE ARE SO MANY THINGS TO DO.
HE CAN CONTEMPLATE THE WAVES,
LOOK FOR SHELLS,

TAKE A NAP, ENJOY THE MOMENT,

TEACH HIS FRIENDS HOW TO SWIM,

TO TELL THE TRUTH, THERE'S SOMETHING THAT'S
BEEN GNAWING AT HIM, BOTHERING HIM,
AND STRESSING HIM OUT.

FOSSIL IS SCARED

TO GO IN THE WATER.

IMPOSSIBLE!

CROCODILES AREN'T SCARED OF ANYTHING!

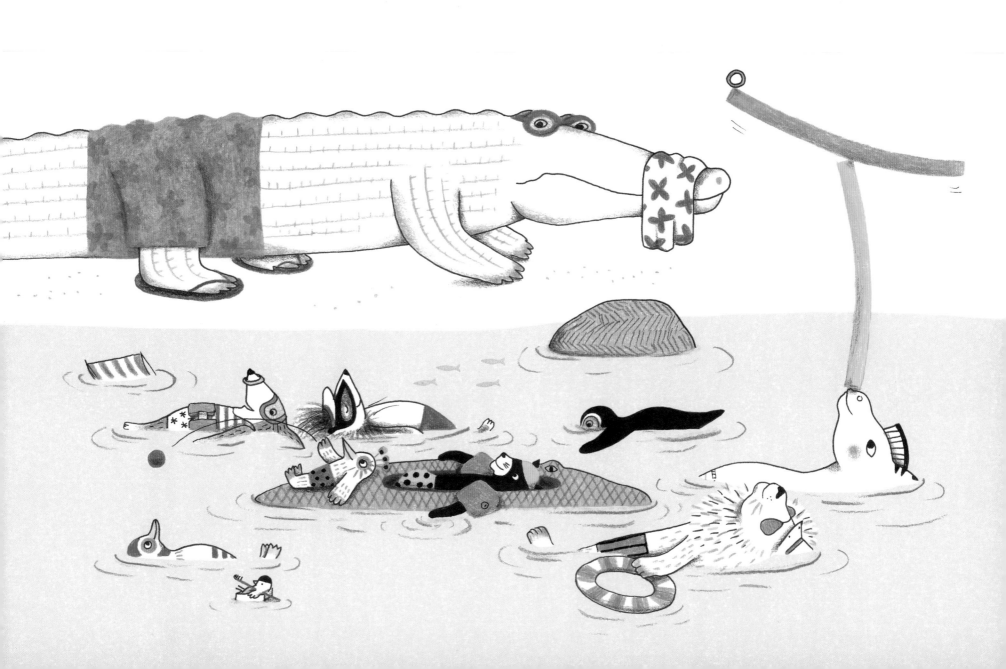

ESPECIALLY THE WATER!

FOSSIL, DON'T BE AFRAID.

THERE ARE FLOATIES.

COME ON!

BELIEVE US, IT'S NOT THAT BIG OF A DEAL.

SPLASSSHHH

FOSSIL THE QUIET CROCODILE LOVES THE BEACH,
ESPECIALLY WHEN THE TIDE IS LOW...
AND ALL HIS FRIENDS ARE WITH HIM.

FIPPO, THE HIPPO

SONNY, THE BUNNY

RYAN, THE LION

MOOMOO, THE COW

SHERRY, THE SHEEP

ZOG, THE DOG

ZACHARY, THE ZEBRA

RUBYLETTE, THE BIRD IN RED

MYRTLE, THE TURTLE

TEDDY, THE BEAR